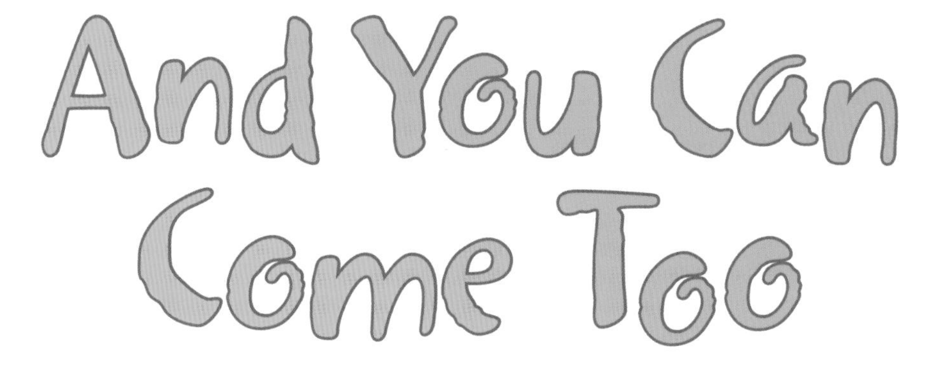

And You Can Come Too

Ruth Ohi

Annick Press

Toronto • New York • Vancouver

Cover and interior design: Sheryl Shapiro and Ruth Ohi

Annick Press Ltd.

We acknowledge the support of the Canada Council for the Arts, the Ontario Arts Council, and the Government of Canada through the Book Publishing Industry Development Program (BPIDP) for our publishing activities.

Cataloging in Publication

Ohi, Ruth
And you can come too / Ruth Ohi.

ISBN 1-55037-905-4 (bound).—ISBN 1-55037-904-6 (pbk.)

I. Title.

PS8579.H47A64 2005   jC813'.54   C2005-901329-X

The art in this book was rendered in watercolor.
The text was typeset in Humana Sans.

Distributed in Canada by:
Firefly Books Ltd.
66 Leek Crescent
Richmond Hill, ON
L4B 1H1

Published in the U.S.A. by:
Annick Press (U.S.) Ltd.
Distributed in the U.S.A. by:
Firefly Books (U.S.) Inc.
P.O. Box 1338
Ellicott Station
Buffalo, NY 14205

Printed in China.

Visit us at: www.annickpress.com

For Kaarel, with love
—R.O.

On Saturday, Sara and Annie played together all day and did not fight, not even once.

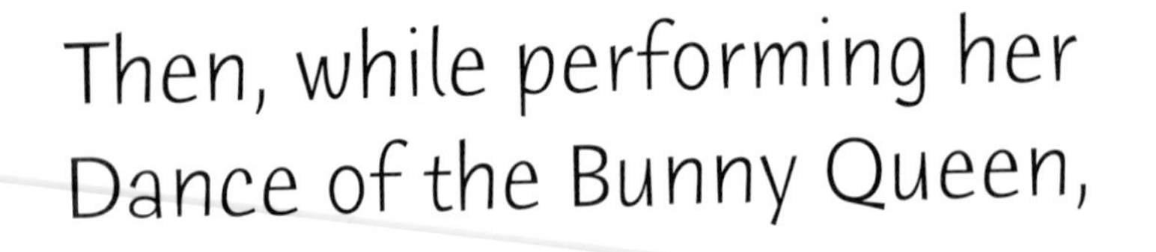

Then, while performing her
Dance of the Bunny Queen,

Annie accidentally bumped
Sara's Fortress of Doom.

So Sara pushed her.

Daddy was walking by with the laundry.

"Sara," said Daddy gently,
"we don't push in this family."

“You don’t love me!” said Sara.
“I do love you, Sara,” said Daddy. “Very much.”
“I’m running away!” said Sara.

"Annie loves Sara," said Annie.
Sara packed. She needed six bags.

“All right,” said Sara. “You can come too.”

"Would you like me to set up a tent for you?" asked Daddy.

"Yes, please," said Sara.

Daddy brought out a
blanket and a very long rope.
It rained, but only briefly.

There was a rustle in the bushes and
Daddy turned to see what it was.

"Don't worry, Daddy," said Sara. "I'll protect you." Sara let out her loudest roar.

"All gone!" said Annie.

"It's getting late," said Daddy. "Would you like your flashlights?"

"Yes, please," said Annie. "Bear needs a night light."

"I'm getting hungry," said Daddy. "Would you like a cheese sandwich?"

"Yes, please," said Sara. "With the crusts cut off."

"I'm getting sleepy," said Daddy. "Can I read you a story before falling asleep?"

"Yes, please," said Sara, yawning.

They read until bedtime.

The stars came out.

And so did Mommy.